DATE DUE

DEC 1 2 1983	DEC 2 1 1993	JAN 0 5 2008
JAN 2 0 1984	JAN 0 9 1995	
DEC 2 8 1984		
DEC 1 4 1984	MAR 6 1995	
DEC 2 8 1985	DEC 2 0 1995	
DEC 2 8 1985	DEC 2 8 1996	DEC 2 2 2006 JAN 1 2008
DEC 18 1987		JAN 0 3 2015
JAN 4 1988	DEC 2 4 2003	
DEC 2 3 1988	MAY 0 1 2004	
MAR 3 1 1980	JAN 0 3 2005	
NOV 1 1 1989		
JAN 4 - 1990	DEC 1 5 2005	
JAN 1 6 1991	DEC 1 6 2006	
DEC 1 6 1991	JAN 0 9 2012	
FEB 1 0 1992	JAN 0 2 2014	
DEC 2 8 1992	DEC 2 1 2015	
JAN 1 3 1993		

Where's Prancer?

Story and pictures by SYD HOFF

HARPER & ROW, PUBLISHERS, NEW YORK, EVANSTON AND LONDON

It was early in the morning when Santa
Claus returned to the North Pole after
his big trip all over the world.

"I'm tired and I guess you are, too," he said to the reindeer. "So suppose you get to the stable and I'll see you all later."

Santa went into the house and had a
nice hot cup of tea.

Then he put eight fresh carrots in a basket and took them out to the stable.

"Here, Dasher, Dancer, Prancer and Vixen," he said. "Here, Comet, Cupid, Donder and Blitzen—here's a nice carrot for each of you."

There was one carrot left over!

"One reindeer is missing," said Santa.
"Who is it?"

"It isn't I," said Dasher.
"It isn't I," said Dancer.
"It isn't I," said Vixen.

"It isn't us either," said Comet, Cupid, Donder and Blitzen.

"It's Prancer," said Santa.
"Where can he be?"

"He was with us in Australia,"
said Dasher.
"He was with us in Sweden,"
said Dancer.
"He was with us in the Philippine
Islands," said Vixen.

"He was also with us in Sioux City, Iowa," said Comet, Cupid, Donder and Blitzen.

"Keep thinking, boys," said Santa. "If we don't get Prancer back, there may never be another Christmas. Everybody knows I have to have eight reindeer."

The telephone rang.
"Maybe it's Prancer!" cried Santa.

It was only a wrong number.

There was a knock on the door.
"Maybe it's Prancer!" cried Santa.

It was only a walrus knocking ice off his flippers.

"We remember," said the reindeer. "It was Philadelphia. That was the last place we saw him."

"Quick, to the sleigh!" shouted Santa. "There isn't a second to lose!"

In the twinkling of an eye they were in
the City of Brotherly Love.
"Spread out now and look," said Santa.

Dasher went up Market Street but all he saw was a cat.

Dancer went up Broad Street but all he saw was a dog.

Vixen went into Fairmount Park but all
he saw was a squirrel.

Comet and Cupid met at Independence
Hall.

"A fine structure," said Comet.

"Yes," said Cupid, "but where's Prancer?"

"Here he is!" shouted Donder.
"That's only your reflection," said Blitzen.

A police car drove up. "A reindeer was just reported on Chestnut Street. Did you lose one?" asked the policeman. "Yes," said Santa. "Thank you. We'll go get him."

Sure enough there was Prancer.

"Where have you been?" said Santa.
"We were worried about you."

"I just wanted to see how people look on Christmas Day," said Prancer. "We always get here the night before."

"Let's all see," said Santa.

They saw many happy faces and were glad they had helped make them that way.

Then Santa said: "Now we must go home."

Prancer sat with Santa and enjoyed the ride.

Once more Santa made himself a nice hot cup of tea and once more he took eight fresh carrots out to the stable.

This time there was none left. "Merry Christmas," said Santa.